To Bella – Sweet dreams.

An Imprint of Sterling Publishing
387 Park Avenue South
New York, NY 10016

ISBN 978-1-4351-4754-6

Manufactured in Johor, Malaysia.
Lot #:
2 4 6 8 10 9 7 5 3 1
02/13

Bedtime Without ARTHUR

Jessica Meserve

Sandy Creek
NEW YORK

Bella has a bear.
A very special bear called Arthur.

He is as brave as a knight.
He is as **strong** as ten elephants.

And he does karate.

When Bella sleeps,

Arthur
is
BUSY.

He guards the bed and keeps
away monsters that come
sneaking from the shadows.

Safe in her bed,
Bella dreams
of her favorite things,
like rainbows
and rainforests.

One morning, Arthur was worn out from so much karate.

Bella made him his favorite breakfast of toast and honey, and then tucked him up snug in bed.

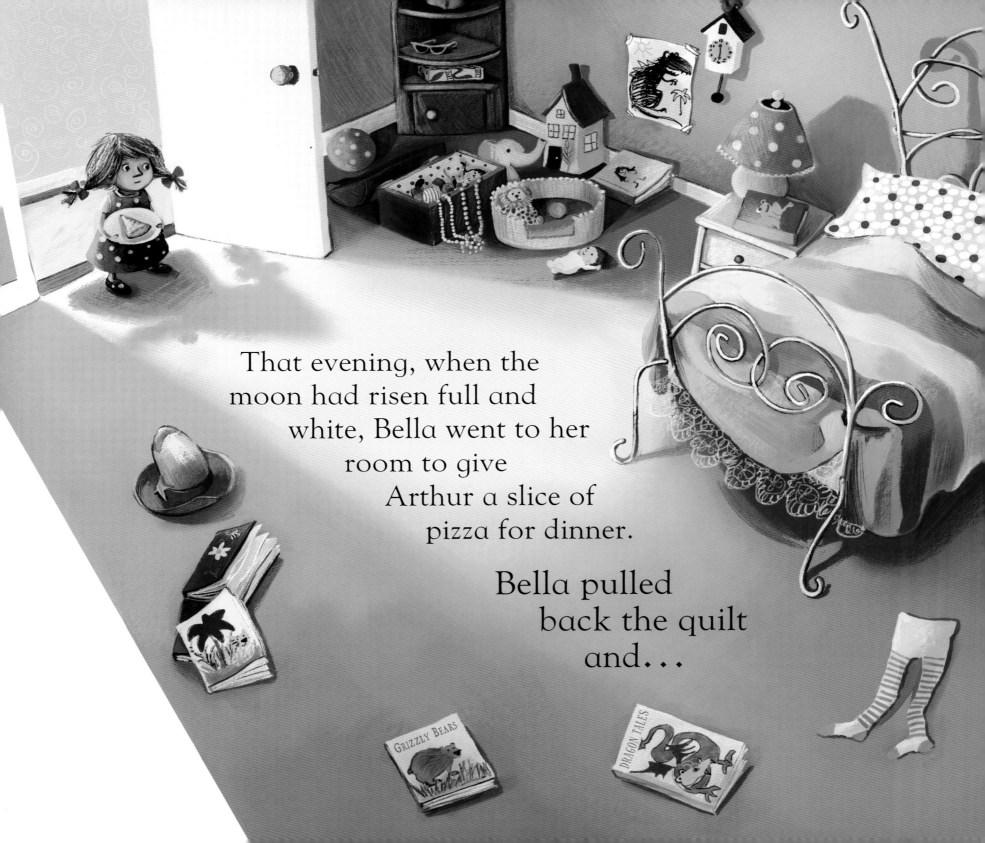

That evening, when the
moon had risen full and
white, Bella went to her
room to give
Arthur a slice of
pizza for dinner.

Bella pulled
back the quilt
and...

...yowled,

"Arthur!"

He was gone.

Bella searched

and searched.

Bella's mom looked upstairs.
Bella's dad looked downstairs.
Bella's brother, Freddy,
looked worried.

None of them could find Arthur
ANYWHERE.

Mom said, "We'll find him tomorrow."

Dad said, "He'll turn up."

Freddy said, "Sorry."

But Bella didn't believe them.
Her lip trembled as she
climbed into bed.

Bella couldn't sleep.
She was sure there were
MONSTERS
watching and waiting.

Bella squeezed her eyes tight shut.
She fell asleep dreaming of

FIRE-BREATHING DRAGONS,
SLUGS,
and grizzly bears.

In the morning, Bella
was exhausted.

She couldn't juggle.

Even the ice cream didn't cheer her up.

And at bedtime there
was still
no sign
of Arthur.

The wind began to

blow and howl.

Bella woke with a start.

She saw things
looming and
scratching at
the glass.

Bella leapt out of bed and ran as fast
as she could across the hallway
into her brother's room.

Freddy was sound asleep.
Bella began climbing
into his cot.

Peeking from under the blanket, she
saw the tip of a soft, furry nose.

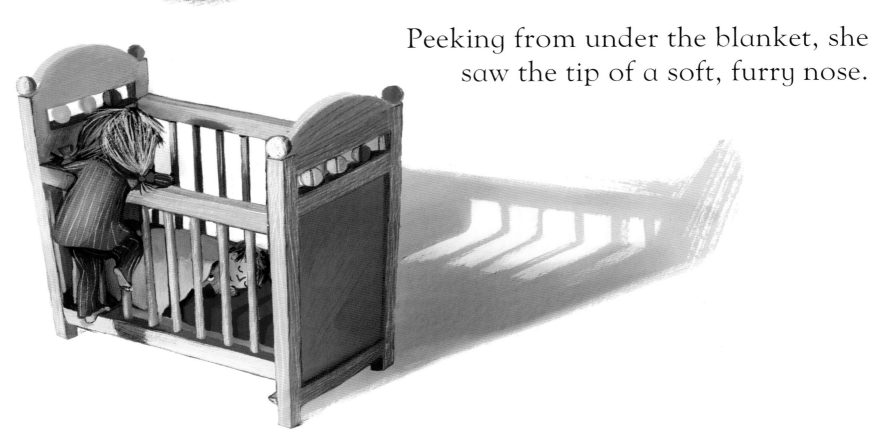

It was Arthur!

Bella was **so** happy to see him . . .

. . . but she was
very angry with her
brother for taking him.

She grabbed Arthur and headed back to her room.

Left all alone, Freddy was afraid.
"Monsters!" he cried.
Bella pretended not to listen.

"Serves him right," she thought
as she reached the door.

Bella looked back at her brother.
She saw Freddy's eyes, wide and full of tears,
and her anger melted away.

Bella realized that Freddy needed Arthur more than she did. Freddy wasn't nearly as strong and brave as she was.

Bella took Arthur back to Freddy and tucked them both up in bed.
"Don't be scared, Freddy. Arthur will look after you."

Bella felt braver and
braver with each
step she took back
to her room.

When at last she climbed into
bed, Bella felt as brave as a
knight. All the monsters shook
with fear and fizzled into nothing.

That night Bella slept long and deep, and dreamt of all her favorite things.

And so did Freddy.